I Can Pat

HAILEY SCRAGG

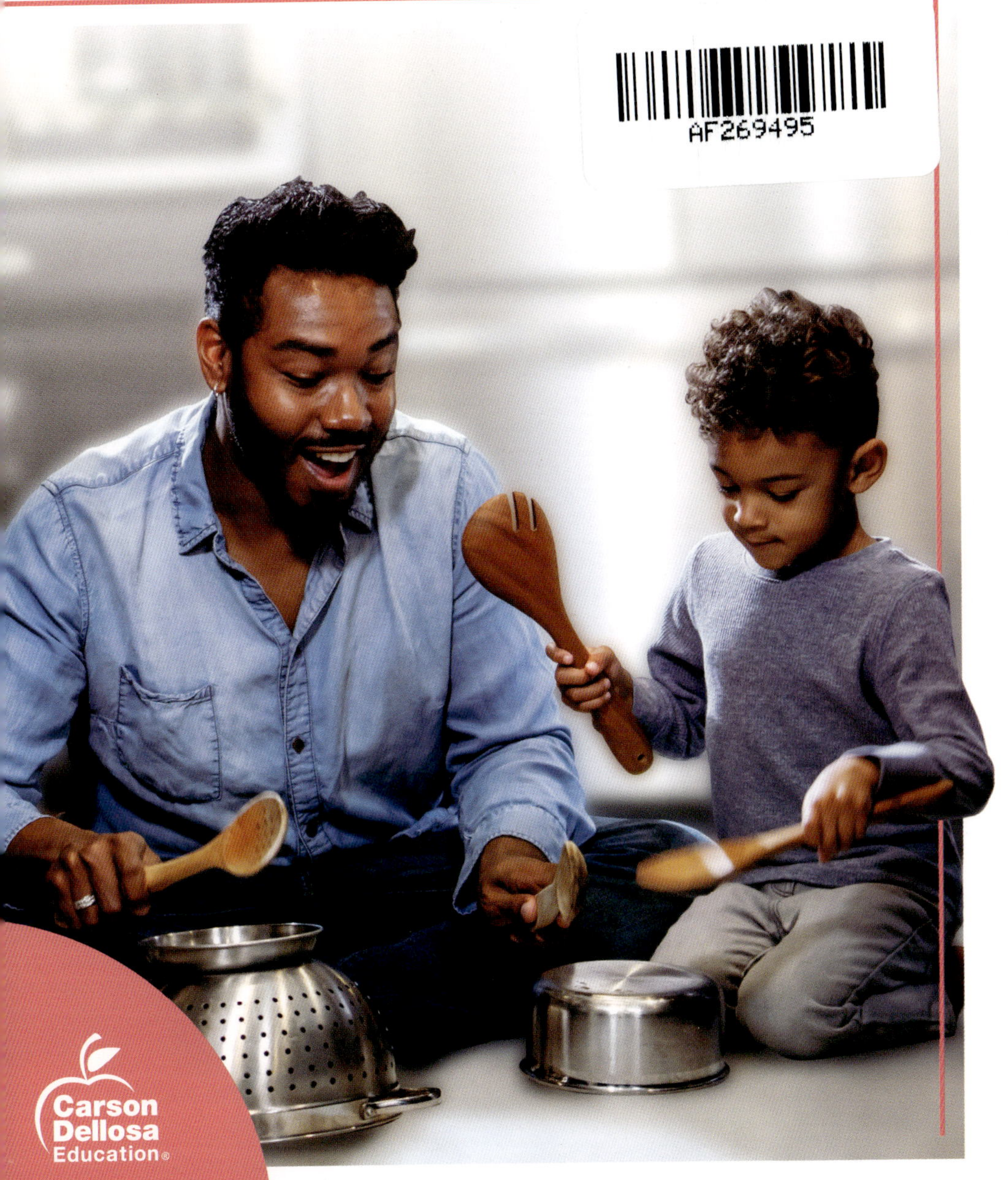

I can pat a cat.

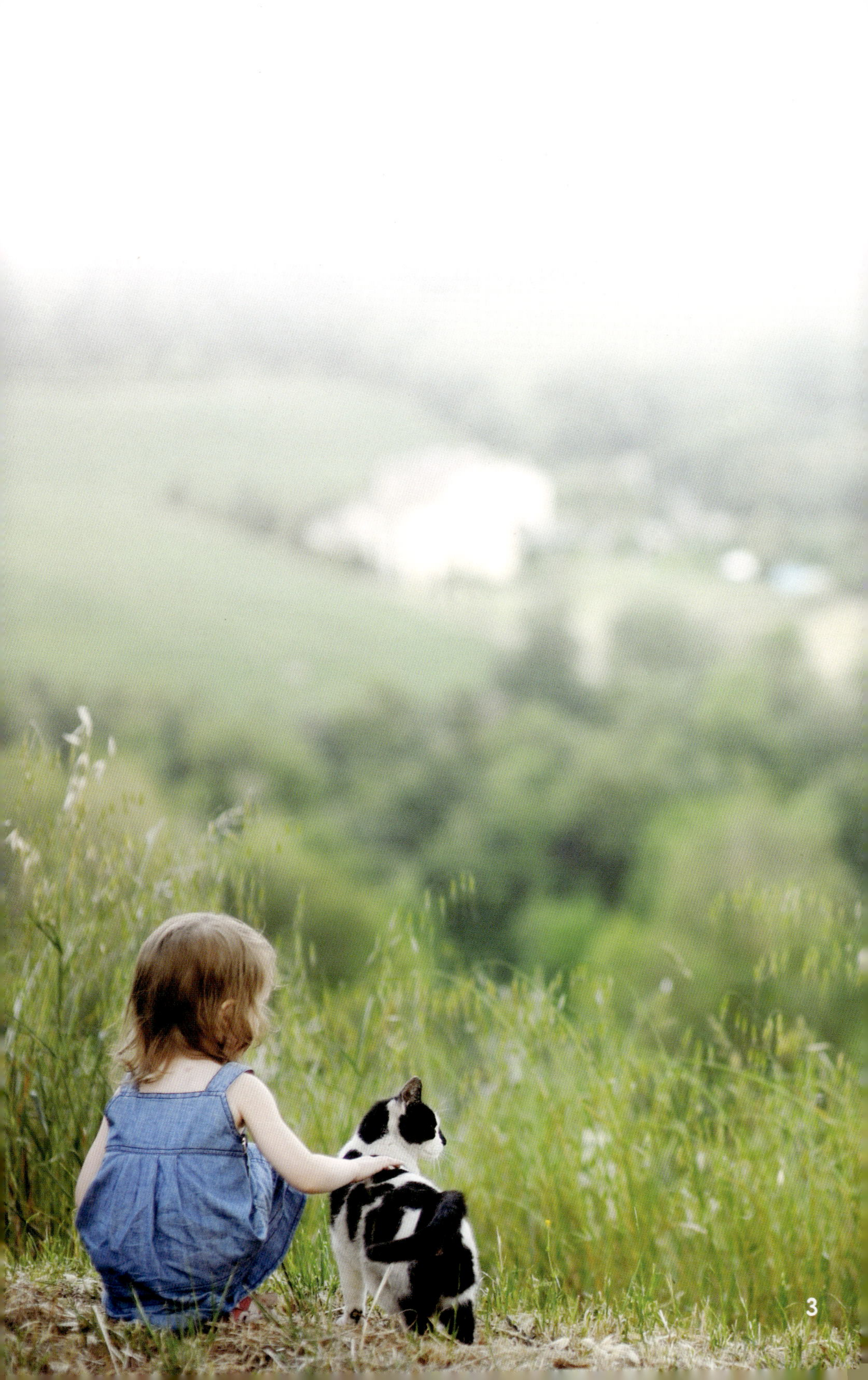

Not this cat!

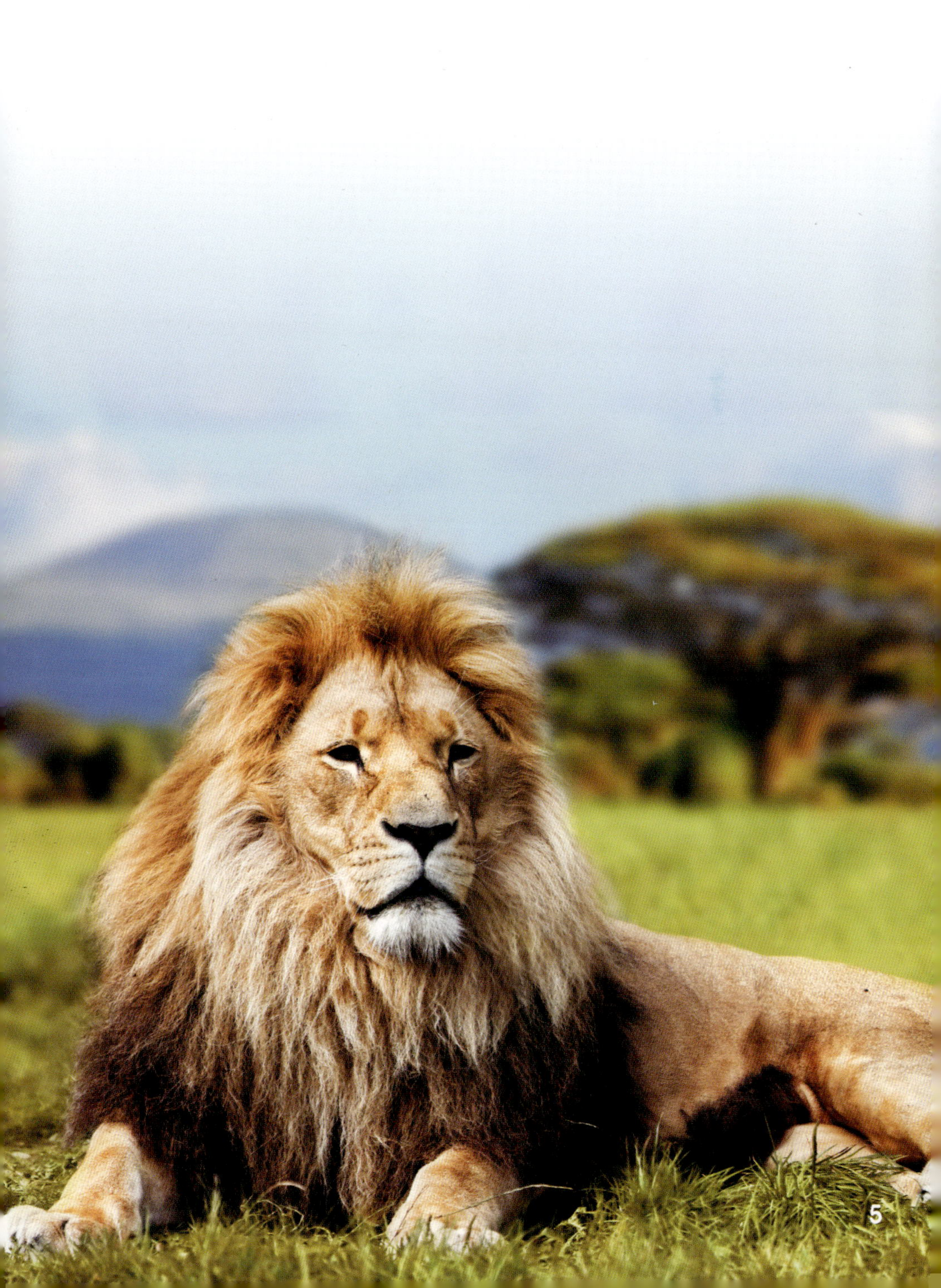

I can pat a hat.

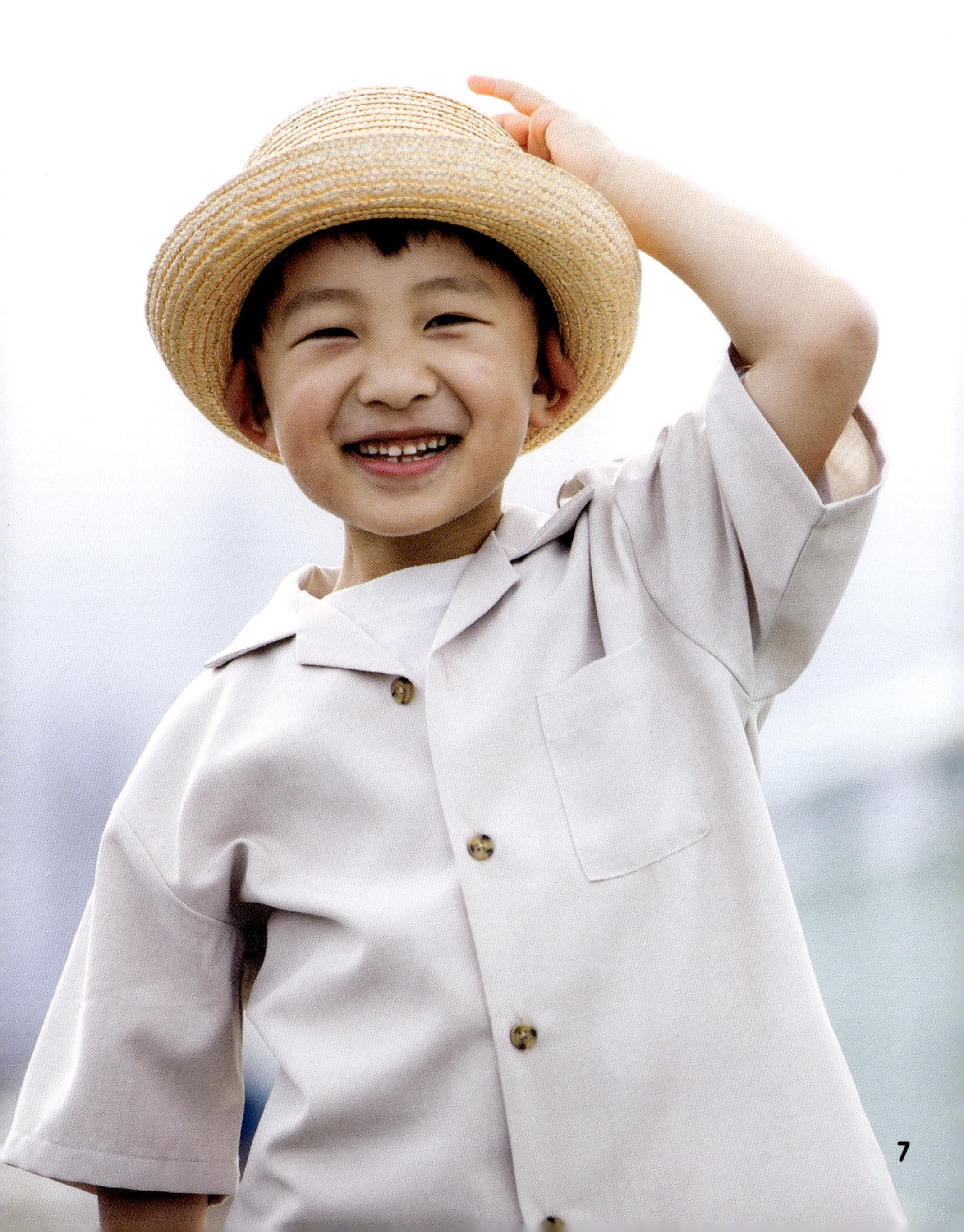

Not this hat!

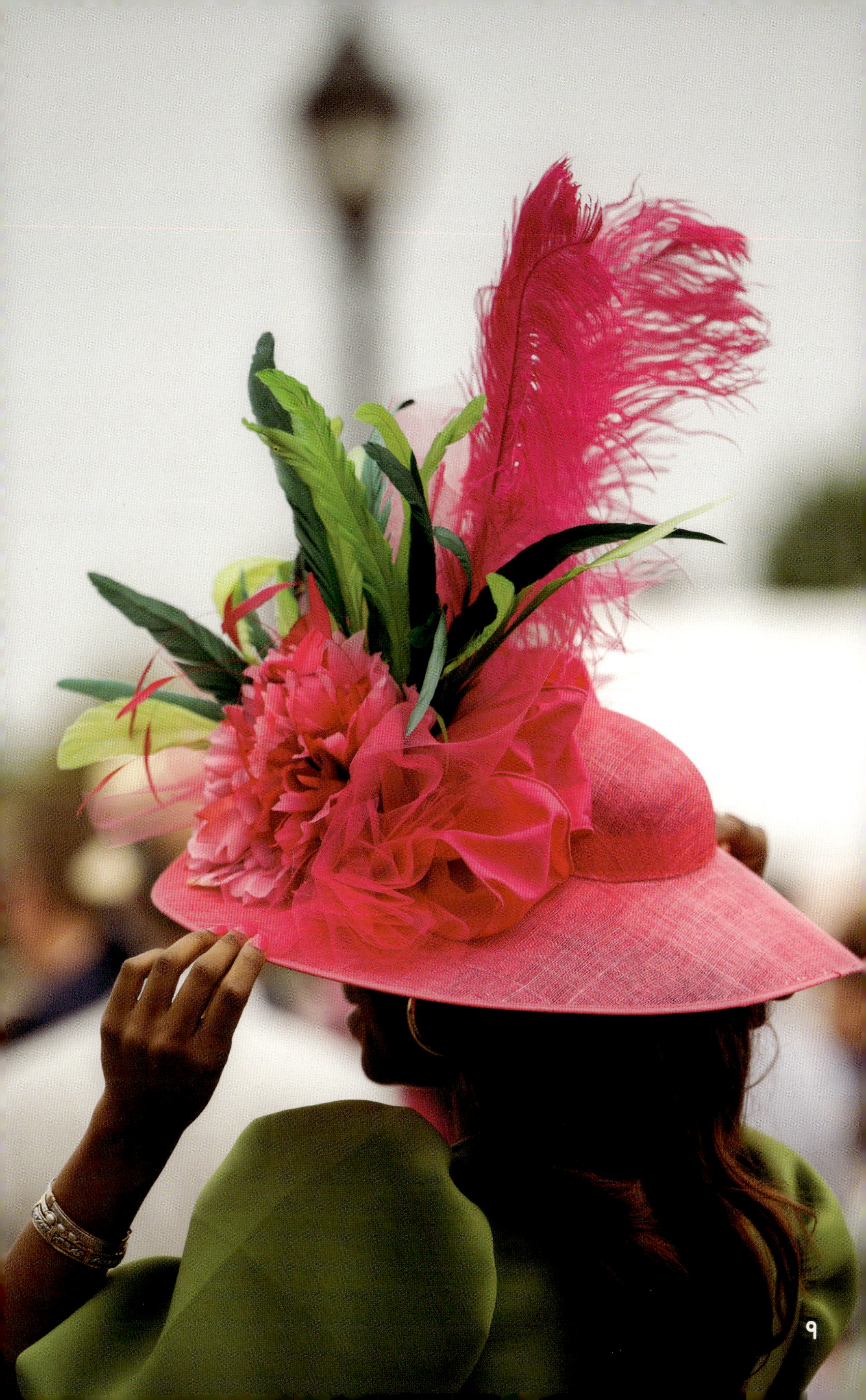

I can pat a bat.

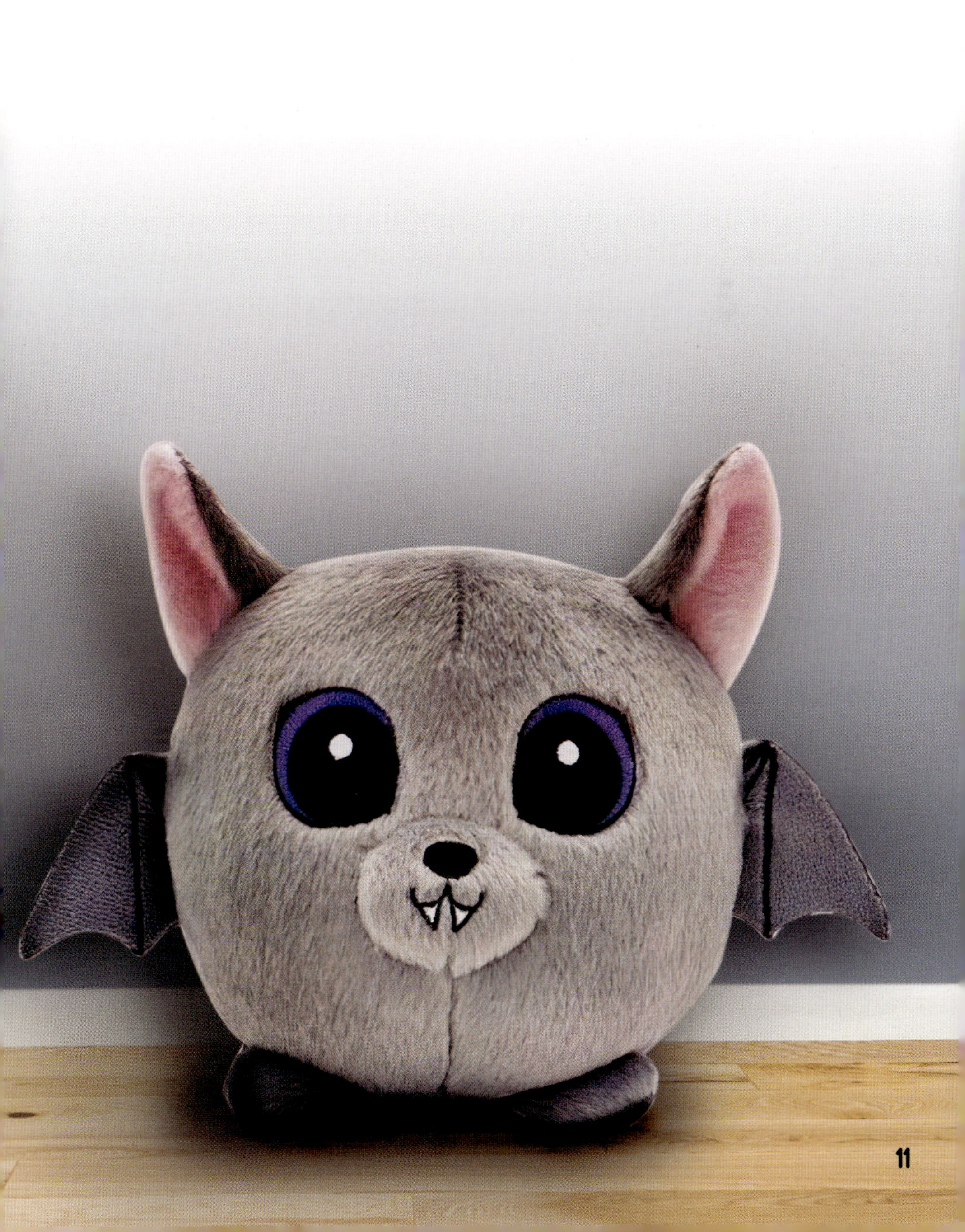

Not this bat!

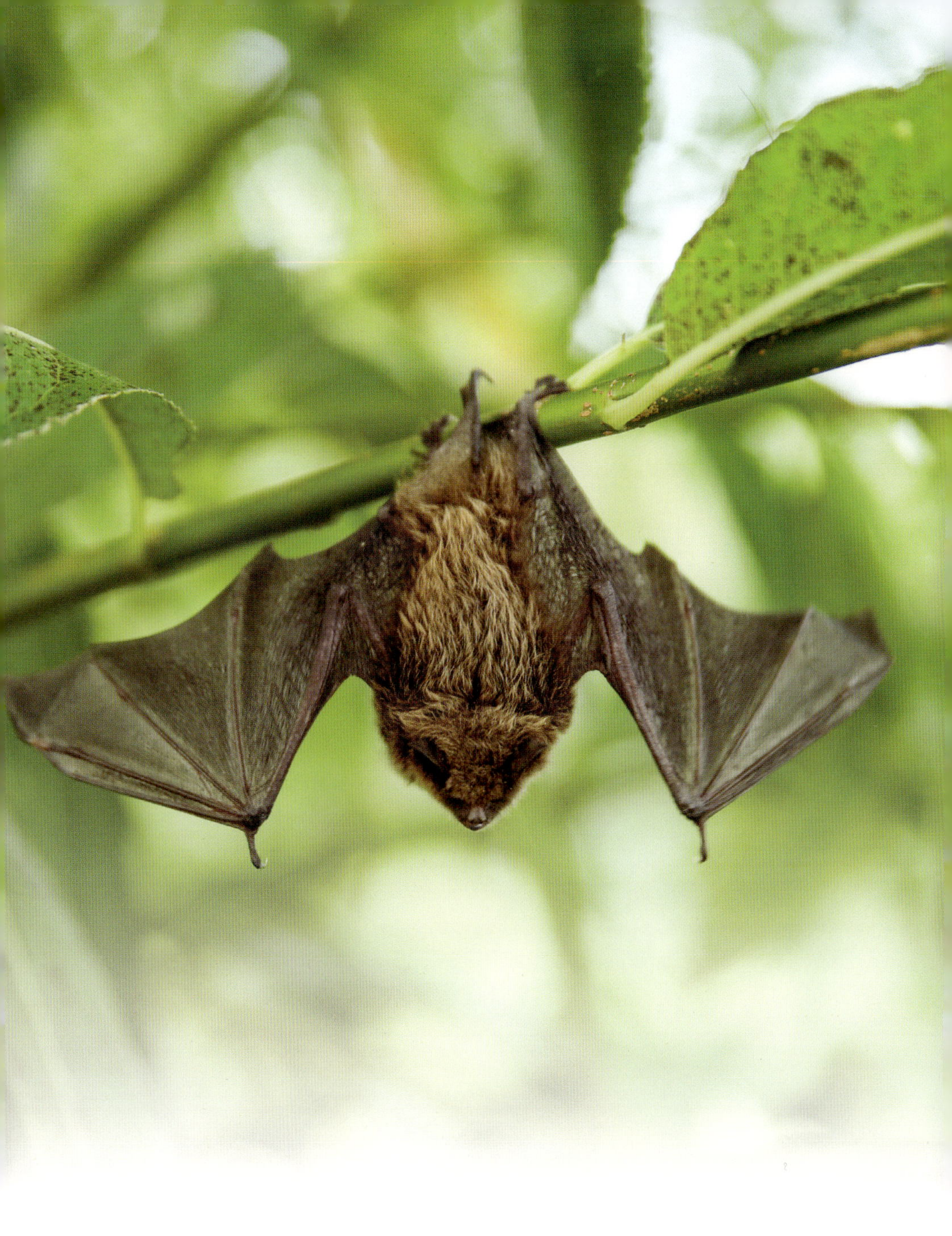

I can pat a pan.

I can tap.

I can jam!

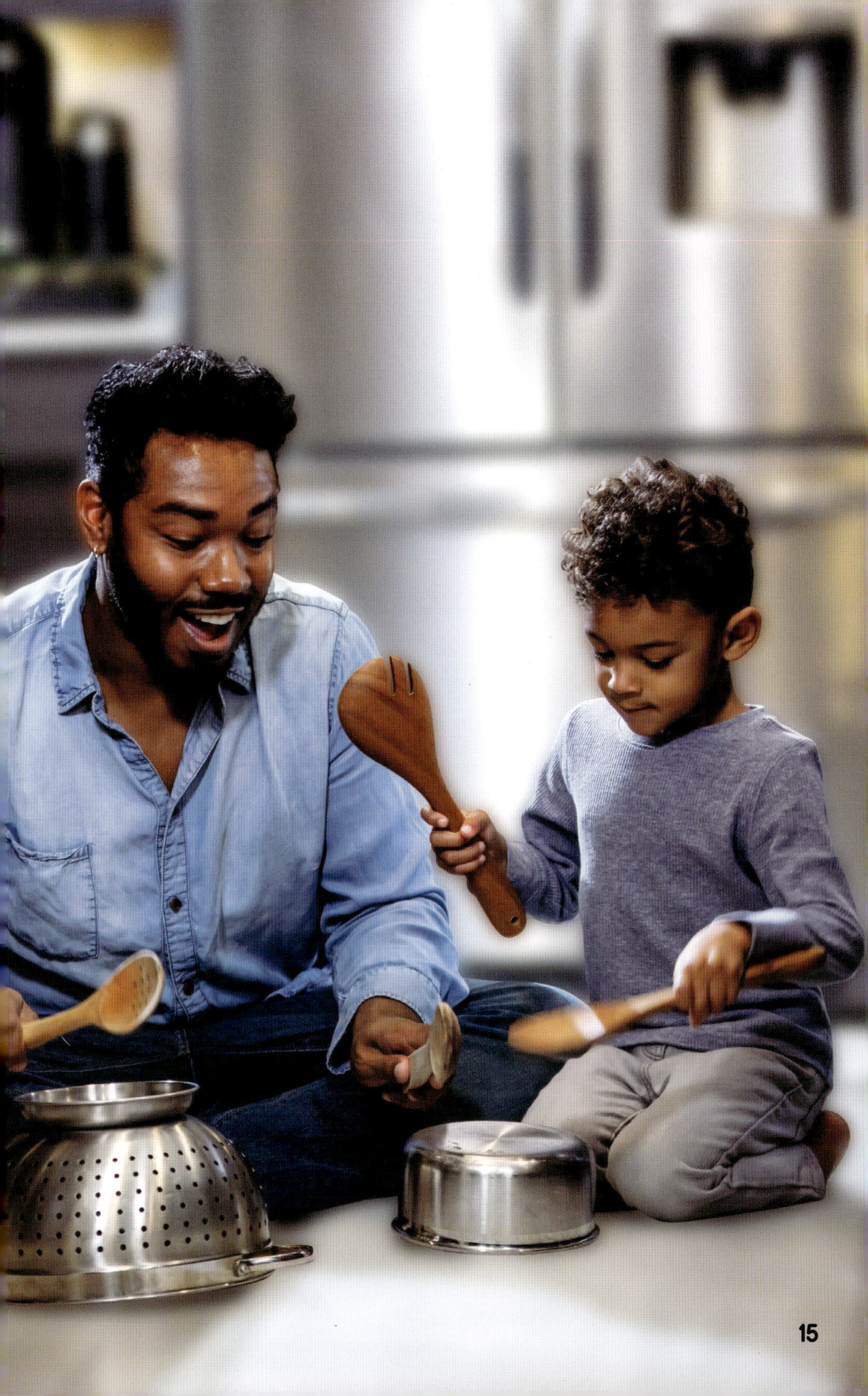

bat	hat	pat
can	jam	tap
cat	pan	

High-Frequency Words

a	not
I	this